DRATHER'S STORY

an Expired Reality novella

David N. Alderman

ISBN: 978-1-945712-39-5

Visit **DavidNAlderman.com**

Chapter 1

A Happy Birthday

Tuesday, December 18th, 1990

The cold wind on the night of his eighteenth birthday ripped at Jonathan Huxley's bare skin like hounds' teeth, pulling at the small hairs on his arms and the back of his neck, threatening to tear him apart. His nose reddened with the cold, and his eyes watered, making it hard to see the bottom of the trash can he was bending into.

The dim light from the streetlamp cast its eerie glow across the otherwise dark alley, while gusts of wind moved the light pole back and forth with an uncanny creaking sound.

Jonathan pulled himself out of the trash can, half of a rotten banana dangling from his frostbitten fingertips. He placed the fruit on the ground for a moment while he struggled with the frozen zipper on his jacket, trying to get it up to his chin. The coat had holes in it to begin with, making it easy for the pins of chilly air to sneak in and attack him here on the streets of Mecca. He managed to get the zipper up and then quickly shoved his fingers into his mouth to warm them up. The taste of banana, stale coffee, and wet chewing tobacco coated his taste buds, forcing him to spit toward the can.

1

He glanced down to see where he had put the banana and watched a large rat scurry toward him, grab the banana peel in its mouth, and take off down the alley, into the darkness, safe from the faint glow of alley light.

Jonathan cursed under his breath, angry that he had sought that prized item for the last hour and had been so foolish as to place it on the ground.

He kicked the garbage can, watching with some satisfaction as it fell over and vomited its contents across the dark puddles in the asphalt. That was the last trash can he was willing to search through this evening, so he accepted the fact that he was going to have to go without food today. The last item he ate was half of a stale turkey sandwich coated in some white sauce, which he guessed had been rotten milk, for dinner the night before. This meant he would have to find food in the morning or he would be in danger of starving.

He walked out of the alley and into the streets. The bright, neon lights of the closed shops glistened under the spell of the midnight hour. Up above him, a thick fog blocked the moonlight from reaching that level of the city. Jonathan walked hastily, hoping nobody had taken over his home for the evening. He was tired and hungry, but fatigue overrode the urgency to eat.

He passed by another alley, the last he would see until he reached his destination. Down at the end of the alley, stood a couple of tall figures surrounding a female in a violet-colored dress. She was backed up against the wall, her arms in front of her in defense to whatever they were trying to do to her. He shook his head and moved on, knowing it would not be wise to sacrifice his own life for another's, especially in this cold. He already learned that harsh lesson once, and that was enough to deter him from attempting it again.

He reached an abandoned cement staircase that led down to a grimy door. He glanced around the area to make sure nobody was watching him and then pulled out an iron key, which he used to unlock the door that led into a wide, well-lit stairwell. He shut the door behind him and locked it, finding some warmth in the empty space.

The key was a mystery to him, given by a complete stranger who was wandering the streets like Jonathan only a few weeks ago. Jonathan was extremely grateful to the cloaked female but had been unable to find her again to thank her for her generosity. Generosity was a currency not easily found here in the "bottom docks" as they were called, the slums of the inner city.

He made his way down a flight or two of the silver-painted stairs and sat in the corner of the landing. The sounds of the large gears a few flights down would lull him to sleep in no time, as they had each night over the past few weeks. He loved the click and clack of the large gears, the city's energy generated by their perpetual movement.

His eyes slowly sank lower as his mind replayed events of the day in a blurry, jagged stream of consciousness. It was his birthday today, wasn't it? He couldn't remember all that well. A stale banana was all he got? Was he eighteen now? *Yes.* How long had he been on the streets? He couldn't recall. Was the woman in the violet dress okay? *She won't be for long.* How long had he gone without someone to celebrate his birthday with? In his drowsiness, all he could remember from his childhood was a large, circular angel food cake that his mother had plastered with chocolate frosting and topped with ten birthday candles. He had blown them all out with a single breath but never got his wish. His mother had given him a birthday kiss on the cheek…

Jonathan succumbed to sleep in a matter of minutes.

Each night he dreamed of the same things, scattered along the plain of his subconscious differently: the many alleys he had scrounged through, the bits and pieces of food he found himself shoving down his throat each day, the women dressed in slutty outfits, giving their bodies over to poverty and every type of sexual activity. Every now and then, he would dream of his parents, or what he could remember of them. They passed away when he was ten, so his memories of them were faint, but they were good memories and they warmed him on dark, cold nights such as this.

Every morning, the city gears sounded a little bit louder, as if raising their voices at the sight (or thought) of dawn on the topside. They woke him around the same time each day, dragging him out of his dreams and into the real world again— a world he didn't really want to wake up in.

He opened his eyes, and depression hit him. He quickly attempted to push it out of his mind and heart, having learned how to control his emotions to a decent degree. Usually if the streets didn't kill someone, the insanity of living on them would. He wasn't going to let that happen to him. He wanted to make something of himself someday, not die down here in the slums or cave into becoming a professional thief.

He shuffled out of the corner and strained to get to his feet, the gears louder than ever now. He stopped and listened for a moment, noticing another sound other than just the gears. Someone was pounding on the door at the top of the stairwell. His mind raced. If it was the police, they weren't going to be kind to him, not if they found him down here. Tinkering with the city's gears was cause for imprisonment and most times, from what he heard, death.

His gaze wandered down the stairwell, down to where the soft glow of lighting merged into darkness. He knew he couldn't escape down there. Rumors ran rampant through the streets about unmentionable things that occurred to those who wandered into the gear rooms. He heard of creatures there that didn't want to be disturbed and would make a meal out of you if they were. He could have sworn he could smell rotten flesh wafting up from the shaft while he mused about these awful things.

He shook his head as the knocking quickened. He knew he better open the door. Infuriating the police wasn't the smartest thing to do.

He climbed to the top of the stairs and unlocked the door, swinging it open to a figure covered in blue armor. An Anaishan sentry. His giant blue helmet and blue face shield glimmered in the morning light breaking through the dispersing fog.

"Jonathan Huxley?" a mechanical voice questioned from the helmet.

Jonathan still wasn't sure if these sentries who patrolled the streets were human or mechanical robots.

"Yeah?"

The sentry moved to the side to reveal an older gentleman in a black tweed overcoat. Gray hair covered his face. He wore a tall hat and carried a cane in his left hand. All of his weight seemed to be pressed on that cane, causing him to lean to the left a little.

"Who are you?"

The old man scowled. "Do not speak to me, boy, until I have spoken to you. That is the rule of age."

"Who are you?"

"Hmph." The old man turned to the sentry and nodded. "Thank you. I will take it from here."

The sentry stared at them for a moment, then turned and left.

The old man turned back to Jonathan and sneered. "Listen, young man. Listen very carefully to me because I will not repeat myself, not even once. I am going to give you the opportunity of a lifetime. I am going to give it to you once. If you decline, you will not have a chance at this again. Not by me, and I certainly doubt you will get another chance by another individual as generous."

"You still haven't answered my question. Who are you?"

"My name is Reginald Arthur the Third."

"Who?"

"To you, it shouldn't matter."

"You're right. What do I care who you are?"

"Hmm. Disrespectful, are we? I guess that can be attributed to your time on the streets since your parents died."

Jonathan glared at him. "What do you know about my parents?"

"I know much, but that knowledge is not relevant at this point in time. The offer I am going to make to you is simple. I will take you into my home and provide food, shelter, all of the amenities you could possibly desire. All in return for one thing."

Jonathan stared at the man, watching him shift his weight to the right a little.

"I want you to marry my friend's daughter in a week's time, to secure the legacy of my family."

Jonathan laughed. "Yeah, right. That's what you want from me? To get married?"

The man nodded. "You have approximately one minute to make your decision. After this minute, which has already started, if you have not made your decision, I shall leave this place and you will never hear or see me again."

"How can you expect me to make a decision like this that quickly?"

"You are homeless, boy. What is there to decide? I told you

what I am offering. You have fifty seconds."

"Who is this girl? Is she attractive? What kinda rules are you going to make me follow while I'm in your house?"

"I am sure, in this case, that your need to survive would greatly outweigh any inquisitive ponderings you may have. I can assure you that this girl is considered attractive in almost every circle through which she has passed. *Who* she is, is irrelevant at this point in time. And of course, as with all things in life, there are rules to govern right and wrong. There are no rules that would be outside your capacity to follow, though." He glanced down at his watch. "Thirty seconds. Don't try and convince me that you really have a hopeful life down here in the bottom docks."

"That's a bit insulting."

"So is the amount of time you are taking to accept my generous offer."

"Why do you need me? What makes me so special that you came all the way down here to find me?"

"I need someone to carry on my family legacy. My wife and I cannot have kids together. I already know you are a thief and a liar, so I know what to expect. If I were to adopt from the orphanage, I wouldn't know what or who I would be dealing with. Twenty seconds."

Jonathan thought for a moment. He remembered that thieving rat from the night before, running off with his stale banana. That was his banana. He was tired of digging in the trash, tired of watching women get raped. He was on the brink of becoming someone he didn't want to be just to survive.

He nodded. "Fine."

The old man nodded in reply. "Very well, Jonathan. Come with me, and I will show you your new home and explain the rules of the Arthur household."

Chapter 2

A Charmed Life

As the black limo took Jonathan and Reginald up the long driveway toward the Arthur Mansion, Jonathan gawked at the perfectly cut hedges that lined the driveway. Each one was in the shape of a gem, and each one had leaves of a different color. One represented a ruby. Another, an emerald. Another, a somewhat translucent diamond.

Reginald nodded to the boy. "Those are my favorite things to look at when I come home each day."

"Are the leaves naturally those colors?" Jonathan asked.

"Yes. I had them specially bred. I particularly enjoy looking upon the ruby."

Personally, Jonathan liked the emerald, but didn't say this to Reginald. To Jonathan, Reginald didn't seem like a friendly type, so Jonathan decided to keep his emotional distance from the man. This would safeguard him and help him stay alert and ready in case this guy got out of hand in any way.

The car stopped at a large iron fence. The limo sat, engine humming, as the large black gates swung open automatically. The limo passed through as Jonathan peered out the back window to watch them close. It was like gaining entrance to a castle.

"This is the Arthur Mansion," Reginald said. "It has been in my family for a very long time."

The limo pulled around a half circle and stopped in front of a large fountain with three mermaids, back to back, spitting water into a large stone basin underneath them.

Reginald waited for the driver to open the door, then pressed his cane to the red brick walkway and stepped out of the car. He turned, waiting for Jonathan to come out.

Jonathan couldn't help but gape at the large arch that hovered over the long pathway to the front doors. "This is amazing."

Reginald looked at him with scorn and raised his finger up. "The first rule, my dear boy, is this: This is *my* house. The things in this house are mine and you will not use or touch anything without my permission, which may be granted through asking me for it or by me giving it to you on my own accord. Do you understand the first rule?"

"Sure."

"Dear boy, there is no sure, no maybe, no we'll see. There is only yes or no. That is the next rule: There is only yes or no. Do you understand?"

Jonathan nodded.

"There is no head nodding. There is only yes or no. Do you understand?"

"Yes." Jonathan let the word out like air from a punctured tire. The old man seemed to be getting frustrated, so easily too. Jonathan wondered if he had made the right decision in agreeing to this bargain. He was already starting to miss his freedom on the streets. That little stairwell near the city gears sounded nice right about now, although that infernal rat taking his food surely didn't.

"Follow me, Jonathan." The old man leaned on his cane

once again and started along the red brick pathway that led toward the front doors. They reached the end of the path and the old man turned the door handle, opening the door wide.

Jonathan followed him in. Directly in front of him, a curving staircase led up to a second floor. The walls were all painted white, with colored blocks of glass in random spots. Light shone through the blocks, making them look like different gems, like the hedges outside.

To his right, Reginald pointed out a stainless steel swinging door that led to the kitchen. To his left spanned a very large family room, which Reginald walked him into. Three large couches surrounded a massive television screen embedded into the wall. A statue of a famous pop singer, life-sized, stood to the left of the television.

Jonathan eyed it, noticing the thin and sultry figure of Charm. Her statue had long, brown hair, the strands sculpted perfectly to fall down across her emerald green eyes, the tips barely scraping her breasts.

The old man gave half a smile. "I see you admiring my Charm statue."

"She is…hot."

"Yes, many men think so. I acquired that item from Charm herself when I invested in her record label for her debut album. It was, obviously, a wise investment. She can seduce all the men with her salacious vocals and, at the same time, entice everyone with her wild antics. Quite a talent, if I do say so. Though not things that I personally agree with, Charm's morals and ethics have certainly made me a very tidy profit, of which I cannot complain."

"Oh, Reginald!"

They both looked up toward the stairs where a woman with short, gray hair came stumbling down toward them. She wore a purple silk nightgown and looked as if she had just woken up.

"Jonathan, this is your new mother, Patricia Arthur."

"Oh, sweetie!" She wrapped Jonathan in a massive hug, pressing his face against her bosom. He gasped for air as he tried to struggle out of the hug. She let go of him, and he tripped backward and slammed into the Charm statue. It toppled to the tile floor and shattered.

Jonathan regained his balance and glanced at the mess. He turned back to Patricia and Reginald. Patricia had her hands cupped over her mouth with a look of terror in her eyes. "Oh, dear."

Reginald shook his head, his face turning a quick and dark shade of red. "You foolish imbecile!"

Patricia put her hand on Reginald's shoulder. "Oh, Reggy, go easy on him. He just arrived with us today. He didn't mean to do it. It was an accident."

Reginald grabbed her arm off his shoulder and shoved her backward. She hit the floor. "Shut up! You know better than to give me orders."

He turned back to Jonathan, his eyes raging with fury.

"I—I didn't mean to break your statue. I tripped. It was an accident."

Reginald closed his eyes, taking a deep breath. "Yes, an accident. Of course."

Jonathan nodded, holding his arms out in front of him as if he had some chance to defend himself from an oncoming train. Patricia struggled to stand. He wanted to help her up but seemed to be caught in Reginald's psychotic gaze.

Reginald nodded to him, taking another deep breath before he spoke. "This is the perfect opportunity to teach you another rule, Jonathan. And this is the most important rule of all the

11

rules I will give you, understand?"

Jonathan nodded and then spoke up, remembering the man wanted yes or no answers. "Yes."

"Good. Your next rule, and the most important, is that there are no accidents. Nothing happens just because it happens. There is purpose and reason to everything. All things have odds, and those odds are broken to bring balance to the equations of life. There are no accidents, no mistakes. You either meant to do that or it happened for a reason. The action has to have purpose. It cannot be just because."

Patricia started back up the stairs, grabbing the railing as she pulled herself up the flight. It looked as if she had hurt her back on the tile, but she didn't breathe a word about it.

"Do not concern yourself with her, Jonathan. She is able to take care of herself. She has learned, as you quickly will, that I am the master of this household. Nobody who walks through that door tells me what to do with my house or with the things herein. Do you understand?"

"Yes, sir."

"Very well. I will get Marcel to clean this up. I will show you around the rest of the mansion and then we will get ready for lunch."

***

Reginald gave Jonathan the tour. The building took forty-five minutes to go through, and Reginald made a point only to show Jonathan the important areas, such as the library, the massive garden out back, the basement where Reginald kept most of his collection of artifacts, and all of the bedrooms.

Jonathan thought it funny that Reginald showed him the

artifacts, but then realized that this mansion was probably very well fortified against thieves and monitored from within to prevent anyone on the inside from taking anything out. He had seen no cameras or surveillance equipment, at least no visible signs of any, but knew they were there just the same. Reginald seemed like the type of person who took himself and his family inheritance very seriously.

At the end of the tour, Reginald took Jonathan to his new room on the second floor at the end of a long and vacant hallway. The room was better than Jonathan had expected, with his own bathroom and a window overlooking the garden.

Reginald stood at the doorway of Jonathan's room, staring at him with a look of dismay. "I hope you do not let me down, Jonathan. My family is the most important thing to me. I am hoping that you will find your place in it and learn to take its legacy where I wish it to go."

He nodded. "I will try my best."

"There is a chance that your best may not be good enough, but only time will reveal that. Dinner will be served in the dining area in an hour, so you have time to take a shower and change your clothes."

***

Jonathan didn't know where to start when he saw the set of silverware and dishes in front of him. Reginald and his wife sat there, staring at Jonathan, almost mocking him. Who was he to sit at this table, a table made for the rich? He wasn't rich. He wasn't famous.

He glanced across the table, covered with a red-and-black-striped tablecloth. At the end to his left sat Reginald. At the other end to his right sat Patricia. Jonathan sat in the middle, staring at an empty seat in front of him.

The butler, Marcel Reins, came in through a set of swinging doors carrying a large tray of food.

The tall, gangly man wore a pencil thin moustache that ran across his cheeks and met up with his sideburns. His skin was pale, and he looked quite old. Marcel set the tray down on the table in front of Reginald and waited for him to pick through the different dishes and select what he was in the mood for.

Jonathan glanced down at the silverware again and wondered what utensil to use first. He had two forks, a spoon, and two knives. He felt embarrassed to ask what they were all for, but he didn't want to accidentally spark another lecture on Reginald's rules.

Reginald pointed to a plate of steaming lemon herb chicken. Marcel placed it on the plate in front of Reginald and then headed to the other end of the table to Patricia.

Reginald looked up toward Jonathan, a grimace on his face. "Dear boy, have you never been taught the rules of eating?"

Jonathan shook his head.

"What did I tell you about yes and no?"

Jonathan rolled his eyes and spoke, but it was too late. "No."

Reginald motioned to Marcel. "No dinner for the boy tonight."

The butler smiled. "Very well, sir."

Jonathan cursed under his breath and stood up from the table. "This is ridiculous! I haven't eaten since the day before yesterday!"

Reginald darted up from his seat, his face turning red. "Sit down!"

Jonathan saw the anger boiling in the man's eyes, anger that only moments ago had shown no signs of its presence.

Jonathan glanced to Patricia, wondering if she would intervene. Instead, she picked up her spoon and started to scoop up some of her onion soup.

"The woman will not be assisting you in this matter, boy!" Reginald swung around the corner of the table and stopped a foot from Jonathan's face. "You listen to me. I have come too far in this life to be undone by a young street urchin who has no respect for those who have agreed to take him in and feed him with their kindness."

Jonathan felt his knees trembling with genuine fear. He was certain this man could hurt him. The raw emotion in his tone and demeanor outweighed any physical advantage that Jonathan might have. "I'm sorry."

The man's face turned from red to white almost instantly. He pulled a kerchief out of his suit pocket and wiped his forehead with it. "Very well. Another rule you will be wise to follow is to apologize when you are wrong."

"Yes, sir." Jonathan glanced over to Patricia again, who was sipping her soup without looking up from her bowl. Jonathan sat down, as did Reginald.

Reginald inhaled a deep breath and then took a sip of water. "You and I are going to Lysallis tomorrow on a small business errand. You will accompany me as my assistant and my son, and you will dress the part. First thing in the morning, I will have a suit brought to you. Be up at 6a.m. and we will leave at 8a.m. Is this understood?" The man's eyes looked up from the edge of his glass, waiting for Jonathan's response.

"Yes, sir."

"Very good. Now, Marcel will be by your room at 5:50a.m. to wake you up."

"Yes, sir." Jonathan left to his room without dinner.

Chapter 3

Love in Lysallis

Jonathan had never been to Lysallis, not that he could remember anyway. As their car passed through the center of town, he tugged at the buttoned collar of the shirt Marcel had brought him this morning. He tried to swallow but felt the collar pressing tightly against his Adam's apple. He tugged at the collar some more, trying to make some room for his airway.

Reginald stared at him from the limo seat opposite him. "Young man, stop fiddling with your clothing. That suit is perfectly tailored for you. Now just sit still and enjoy the sights and sounds of the city. We are almost to our destination."

Jonathan did as his guardian requested. He started fidgeting with his hands, traces of black still lingering under his nails from his digs through the trash only a day ago.

The limo pulled into a parking structure underneath a tall blue bank building and parked in a red-lined spot close to the elevators. Reginald motioned for Jonathan to wait. The driver came around and opened the door, allowing Reginald out first. Then Jonathan followed, getting one last tug at his collar before stepping out of the vehicle.

They both took the elevator to the thirty-ninth floor. Reginald stepped out first and motioned for Jonathan to follow him. They headed down a blue hallway and then through a glass door that had the words "Nokei Curiosities, Inquisitor of Fine Antiquities" printed in black on its surface. Red and black carpet lined the inside of the lobby and gave the room a somewhat elegant feel.

Reginald spoke with the receptionist and then turned to Jonathan. "Have a seat. I will be out shortly."

Jonathan nodded and took a seat on the black leather couch. His body practically sunk into it, and he suddenly wanted to sleep. He wasn't used to waking up early, and he knew his body was going to have to adjust if he wanted to please his new guardians.

But then he thought, *Why would I care to please my guardians? Because you were on the streets, you fool,* his conscious berated him in reply. He nodded to himself. Reginald was kind to take him in. He simply had to get used to the man's rules and the order of things around the Arthur residence.

Jonathan glanced around the lobby, taking in the ornate decorations. A large dragon head sat on the dark oak coffee table in front of him, its wooden face painted black and red.

"Would you like something to read?"

The voice sounded heavenly, though at first Jonathan didn't know where it came from. "I'm sorry, what?"

He heard giggling from behind the large receptionist desk. He stood to his feet and walked over. As the other side of the counter came into view, he saw a beauty that amazed him.

Her blue eyes pierced him like barbed spears. "I asked if you wanted something to read."

He shook his head, staring at the woman. Her red hair fell in splashes across her shoulders, half-curls adorning her forehead. She winked at him and then answered a phone call.

He looked away as if he were looking away from the sun. His eyes landed on a painting on the wall opposite him, a painting of a green field with hundreds of red ribbons floating through a blue sky. Dozens of tall trees stood in the background, the green of their leaves glowing with a ghostly radiance.

"I'm sorry. Did you say you wanted something to read?"

Jonathan turned back to her. "Um, no. I'm good."

"What's your name?"

"Jonathan Huxley."

"I'm Rebecca. Rebecca Soft. Was that your dad who went in to see Mr. Nokei?"

"My guardian, actually. New guardian."

She smiled. "An orphan."

He nodded, his cheeks turning slightly red.

"Interesting," she said.

"I'm not sure how."

"I am a very curious woman, Mr. Huxley. I find many things in this world interesting."

His heart beat rapidly just being near her, and he had to remember to control his breathing or he would give away his emotions.

"You okay? It looks like you're breaking a sweat."

He nodded, loosening the tie around his neck. "I'm good."

"Well, I think you're cute, Mr. Huxley. Would you like to take me out sometime? I'll let you buy. Only because it is the gentlemanly thing to do, and you look like a gentleman to me."

He laughed nervously, wiping the sweat off his forehead with the sleeve of his jacket. "I...uh...I would love to."

"You don't sound too sure about it. Am I not attractive to you, Mr. Huxley?"

"Um no...no, that's not it. I just...I just, I am sure. I would love to take you out. Yes, I'll take you out."

She giggled. "I'm just messing with you. You're easy, you know that? Take a deep breath. Relax." She started writing on the back of a business card. "Here's my phone number, Huxley. Call me when you get some time away from your guardian and we'll get together." She handed him the card. "Oh, and I'll pay." She winked at him and smiled with full, red lips.

She had made the zeroes in her phone number as little hearts. He smiled at this, the feeling of her presence washing over him like a cool stream in the desert.

A door opened down the hall, and Jonathan turned to see Reginald saying goodbye to a taller fellow. Jonathan fumbled with the card, trying to shove it into the inside pocket of his jacket as his guardian came toward him. The card slipped in just as he turned to the man.

Reginald stopped and looked him over. "Why are you sweating?" He turned to Rebecca. "Turn the air down in here. You have my poor boy sweating up a storm."

She smiled at Reginald, a smile that almost looked genuine. "Yes, sir. Right away."

Reginald pulled Jonathan along by his shoulder as they stepped back into the hallway and left the tall blue bank building.

***

Jonathan sat in a hotel room in Lysallis that night, staring at the little hearts on the business card. Reginald had gone to another meeting and had left Jonathan to his own doings. Jonathan flipped the card over and saw Mr. Nokei's name printed on the front. Underneath the name, the title, "Inquisitor of Fine Antiquities," was written in raised lettering.

He turned the card back over and picked up the phone to call the girl.

The two agreed to meet at a small mom-and-pop restaurant in the middle of town. Jonathan wore a brown jacket and slacks. Rebecca bested him, though, by showing up in a stunning black dress. Her hair fell in cascades again, this time down her back. She had painted her eyelids green, and she wore the brightest red lipstick he had ever seen.

She grabbed his arm and pulled him into the small restaurant. "Let us dine, Mr. Huxley."

They dined.

Afterward, they took a taxi to the center of town. There they rode an elevator from the bottom of the tall blue bank building all the way up to the top. Rebecca used a lock pick to open the door to the roof. She shook her head at Jonathan when he looked at her curiously. "You don't want to know."

He shrugged, knowing there were a lot of things she didn't want to know about him as well.

They walked to the edge of the roof and stared out at the city around them. Jonathan couldn't remember ever being up this high or being able to look upon a city like this before. The lights of the buildings and the noise of the traffic blended together as if performing a special show for both of them that night.

"Isn't it beautiful?"

He nodded. "It is. I've never seen a city so beautiful."

"This is wonderful," she sighed happily.

"So, how long have you worked for Mr. Nokei?"

She waved the question away. "Oh, please. Aren't we on a date? I want to talk about the stars and the city lights and love…"

Jonathan froze.

She smiled brightly at him. "I'm just kidding, about the love part. I hardly know you, Huxley. And you hardly know me. But I feel a connection to you. Don't misinterpret that as being foolishly head over heels, though. I am a smart girl, and I know the difference between a passing fancy and something lasting. I must warn you, though. I usually get what I want. Only because that is the way you need to treat life. You must reach out and take every moment you can from it, like handfuls of stardust. Whatever falls through the cracks does so because you let it. But each piece of dust you can hold onto is precious."

He gazed on her with a profound respect, not because of her incredible smarts or stunning beauty, but because of her ability to speak to his heart. He nodded, acknowledging her theory on life.

"What do you want from life, Huxley?"

He thought for a moment, turning his body toward the edge of the roof, his eyes staring out on the city. He noticed a tall, neon figure lit up on one of the buildings adjacent to theirs. The building came up to about a quarter of the height of the bank building, and the figure appeared to be a woman in a purple skirt and red halter top. She wore white pigtails, and the letters going down her left side read "Tat's Tats."

He had never been asked what he wanted from life. To be honest, he wasn't even sure.

Rebecca elbowed him gently in the ribs. "C'mon, it can't be that hard of a question. What propels you forward in life? What motivates you? What inspires you?"

He stared into her eyes for a moment, taking in what he could of her. She was a lot, and he wanted every bit of her. He turned his gaze up toward the stars, watching how they twinkled and spread themselves out across the vastness of dark space.

"I guess…I guess I want to know who I am."

"That's a start."

He looked at her, and this time her eyes seemed to call to him. "Yeah, I want to know who I am and…and what my purpose is here on Anaisha." He wanted to tell her about his agreement with Reginald and his wife, but there was no reason to bring it up, right? He detested the thought of ruining this moment.

Rebecca nodded and pressed her lips against his in a mad rush. The moment only slightly caught him off guard and he grabbed her shoulders, pulling her closer to him, taking in her untamed presence.

"Hmph."

They both separated and turned around to find Reginald standing, his cane and his stoic poise overshadowing their rebellious nature.

"Sir?"

"It seems you have much to learn about our agreement, Jonathan. Much to learn."

Rebecca smiled at Jonathan and turned to leave. "I'll find my own way home, Huxley." She waved playfully at him, her eyes never meeting Reginald's.

Jonathan stood there, watching her walk toward the door she had picked open earlier. He felt his heart beating with each step of her confident gait, wanting badly to chase after her. Instead, he turned toward the old man, who was still standing there, glaring disapprovingly at him.

"I am disappointed in you, Jonathan." Reginald made his way to the edge of the building, looking down at the Tat's Tats sign. Jonathan drew to his side as they both faced the city.

"You have agreed to marry in a short time. Don't think I am one of those gentlemen who thinks it is okay to play the field when one is committed to another. My wife and I have been married a very long time, and I would never bring unfaithfulness to our marriage. I hope from this point on you use common sense, dear boy, or it may be the end of you. Tomorrow you will meet your bride, just in time for the wedding this Sunday."

"Yes…sir."

"Listen very closely to me, Jonathan. You are not to see that receptionist again outside of any business ventures I may have in the future with Mr. Nokei, do you understand?"

Though it went against every rebellious cord in his body, Jonathan replied with a yes. He knew his survival was more important at the moment than some fling. But Rebecca had been more than a fling, hadn't she? She was marvelous, with the way she could see Jonathan for who he really was, for the way she spoke unapologetic about everything on her mind and in her heart. The very thought of her made Jonathan smile.

Reginald stared at Jonathan, his eyes cold and calculating. "This is the moment of trust, Jonathan. If you break my trust in you, I will surely repay you the favor."

Jonathan turned and gazed out on the city one last time. The neon lights seemed to have dimmed, and the traffic noise sounded like muffled droning from down below.

Chapter 4

Of Dragons and Mazes

J onathan awoke to Reginald hovering over his bed in the room at the hotel.

"Rise and shine. We have a breakfast meeting with Christina Harbrook—your bride-to-be—and her family in a few hours."

They took the fastest flight out of Lysallis and returned to Mecca, where they rode a limo to a large mansion about fifteen miles from the airstrip. The mansion closely resembled Reginald's, only without the gem bushes in the front. Then again, all the ritzy things were starting to look the same to Jonathan. The limos were all black and long, the mansions were all white and big, the credits were plenty.

A short, older woman in a black-and-white maid's uniform greeted them. She had a glowing gray head of hair that she kept tied in a bun, and her eyes shone with wisdom and wonder. After acknowledging Jonathan and Reginald, she took them to a large table in the dining area, where Jonathan observed five place settings, three of which were already occupied.

The gentleman at the end of the table sat in a wheelchair. To his right sat a woman caked with makeup and wearing a shining blue dress. Her cleavage rose from the top of the dress like the ocean waves in a hurricane. Her smile was painted dark red, and she looked upon Jonathan with hungry eyes as he passed around the table to the seat adjacent to hers.

As he sat, he assessed the younger woman directly across from him. Her hair was tied back in a long ponytail, and she wore a white-and-yellow-checkered dress. She smiled at Jonathan as he settled into his seat.

He smiled back, and that's when he noticed the darkness in her eyes. They seemed to give off an evil energy that made his stomach sour. The stark contrast from the way he had felt with Rebecca the night before left him in a state of mild panic and utter disappointment.

"You must be Jonathan."

He nodded. "I am."

Reginald took the seat to the right of him, across from the mother, who was still staring at Jonathan, her bright blue eyes like those of a wild and unpredictable creature from another planet.

"How are you today?" Christina asked.

"I'm good."

The maid brought out silver trays full of breakfast food for the two guests. Jonathan realized then that the other three occupants of the table had already been eating before he and Reginald arrived.

"I am looking forward to our wedding, Jonathan. Tell me a little bit about yourself."

He glanced nervously at Reginald, who nodded, as if to approve of him telling the truth about his life.

"My parents died when I was ten. I remember little of them. After that, I was forced to live on the streets, where I learned to steal and lie to get what I wanted."

He watched her squirm in her seat, and this gave him some

degree of satisfaction.

"Those days are behind him," Reginald added. "This weekend, you two will marry, and we will all become one big happy family. And, of course, our family heritages will be sealed and secure."

Jonathan looked down at his food and started to pick at the scrambled eggs. His mind wandered back to Rebecca. He enjoyed having her in his head where Reginald couldn't tell him what to do.

"How are you in the sack?"

He looked up from his plate, more shocked when he realized Christina's mother had asked the startling question.

She grinned wildly at him. "Can you please my daughter the way she deserves to be pleased?"

He glanced at Christina, hoping she was also embarrassed by her mother's question. She just stared at him, waiting for his answer. He looked down at the end of the table, to Christina's father, and noticed that the maid was feeding him.

Christina noticed the direction of Jonathan's gaze. "My father was in a traumatic car accident about a year ago, one he almost died in. He's a paraplegic now. He can't move much or talk, and the maid has to feed him and change his diaper."

Christina's mother looked on her husband with disgust, her lips sneering at the sight. "Useless, he is." She turned and saw Jonathan's look of surprise at her comment. "Oh, don't get me wrong. I do love him. But I am at an age where I need to experience life at its fullest, and to be frank, I can't do that with him in this condition."

Jonathan looked back to see Christina sipping her orange juice. She swallowed softly and then looked up at Jonathan. "So, you never answered my mother's question."

"It's a bit of an awkward question to be asking me at the

breakfast table, don't you think?"

Christina and her mother started laughing. Reginald shoved his elbow hard into Jonathan's ribs. He leaned in and whispered in the boy's ear, "Have respect for this family. Don't talk to any of them like that again, understand?"

Jonathan felt sick saying it, but the words, "Yes, sir," fell out of his mouth. He glanced down at his plate and realized he wasn't hungry at all.

Christina took another sip of juice and set her glass down gently on the table. Her movements were slow and deliberate, but there was a glimmer in her eyes, a strange curve to her lips, that told him she had wicked things on her mind. "Jonathan, why don't you join me in a morning stroll through the garden?"

Relieved at the opportunity to get away from the family,— at least part of it anyway—he replied, "That would be nice." He dropped his fork on the plate and followed her to the backyard.

The patio extended about a hundred feet from the house and then stopped at the entrance to a large hedge maze that took up most of the backyard, save for the swimming pool at the other end. Rows of black and white chairs lined the patio, ready for the wedding that would take place in a couple of days.

Christina led Jonathan through the overshadowing walls of hedges, twisted rose bushes, and wild ivy. He found himself pleased by the sweet fragrances of the flowers.

"I know this may be awkward for you, having no knowledge of who I am and having to marry me in a few days."

Jonathan didn't know what to say that wouldn't make her feel bad. "I want to get to know you a little better."

She smiled and grabbed his hand in hers. "And I want to get to know you better." They jogged through the maze to the

27

very center, where a large fountain stood. Four stone dragons posed at different angles near each other, water trickling out of their mouths into a collection of dark blue water below.

Christina sat Jonathan on the edge of the fountain and cupped his hands in hers. "I am going to be totally honest with you, Jonathan, because I believe our marriage needs to be built on trust, in each other and in each other's families. Don't you agree?"

He nodded. "Yes, I do."

"Good. Now, to be honest with you, I don't much care who you are or what you do or where you came from, okay? My goal is to marry into your family to secure a future for me. That's my purpose in taking your hand in marriage. We don't have to love each other or even adore each other. We can just go through the motions and hopefully please each other along the way."

Jonathan's heart sank. Christina spoke about how emotions didn't need to be involved in this "business transaction." While she uttered these words, Jonathan couldn't help but daydream about Rebecca—the wild kiss, that starry night. He felt himself being enveloped by the simple thoughts of her. Where was she right now? Was she working in the office for Mr. Nokei? Was she at home wondering what happened to him? He hadn't had a chance to continue their nighttime rendezvous or even say goodbye for that matter.

"Jonathan? Are you listening to me?"

He broke from his trance and nodded. "Sure."

"Excuse me. Didn't you hear what I said?"

He stood to his feet and stretched a bit, gazing on the fountain of dragons. "Yes, I heard everything you said."

"Then repeat back to me the last thing I said before I had to check if you were paying attention or not."

He shrugged. "What is the point of this? What is the point

of telling me all of this? Can't we try to love each other? Can't we try to make something of this marriage, even if we're both in it just to secure a family heritage?"

She shook her head violently and stood to her feet, her fists clenched at her sides. "Love? Are you crazy? You're a street urchin, Jonathan, definitely not the man I've dreamed of marrying since I was a little girl. You'll do because I need a security blanket. There's no guarantee that I am set for the rest of my life. My father took certain precautions before his accident, barring my mother and me from taking advantage of him if something like this were to happen. Now, I need you to get with the program, okay? Can we just try to make the best of this, in a very professional manner?"

He nodded. "Sure, I'll make the best of it if you will." Jonathan remembered that stale banana and the sleepless nights on the streets and realized this could be much better than that, if he allowed it to be. Besides, he thought hopefully, there might be another opportunity to see Rebecca again…maybe. He quickly dismissed that thought, knowing it was dangerous to be wishing for things like that.

She unclenched her fists and turned from him, crossing her arms. She took a few deep breaths and turned back to him, smiling as she wrapped her arms around his neck and stared into his eyes. He could still see the darkness in her pupils, and it frightened him somewhat.

When she spoke, her breath smelled of oranges. "Listen, Jonathan. You are a lucky, lucky man to get an opportunity like this. To go from living on the streets to living in riches beyond your wildest imagination. You get to marry me, a woman whom millions of men have clamored over. I've had some crazy, unforgettable times in my life so far, and I don't plan on stopping. Even when we marry, I have so many plans to party and travel, to see the world and indulge in my deepest desires."

Jonathan felt his heart sink more. He realized he couldn't let his emotions get too involved in this, especially if she was being honest about her intentions. He knew this marriage was essential to his survival, not just hers and her family's. Someday down the road he could turn around and try to get back out on his own, after he had a good amount of credits in his name. Maybe then he could find Rebecca and pick up where they left off.

"I have to admit, I have been known to be a bit of a wild child, especially since my dad's unfortunate accident."

"Wild child?"

"Drinking, partying...other things." She flashed her teeth at him in a mischievous smile.

Her comment gave way to a brief study of her body: the tight curves where her dress teased him, the way her blonde hair brought out a shimmering glow in her skin, and her smooth legs that tapered down into a pair of black shiny heels.

Jonathan sighed.

It dawned on him with a dreadful truth that his survival would mean putting any thoughts of Rebecca out of his head for good, to leave her in the past, where his parents and his childhood lay derelict.

Chapter 5

The Testing of Loyalty and Spirit

T he next morning, Jonathan awoke in his bed at Reginald's mansion, but he wasn't alone. Christina snored next to him, her long blonde hair spread out across the pillow, her eyes covered in deep, dark eye shadow. He ran his palm across his face and tried to remember the evening before. They had drunk a lot of wine in celebration of their wedding arrangements. He remembered that much.

He shook his head and groaned, remembering a little of what happened between him and Christina late into the night. He turned out of the bed, careful not to wake her up. He wanted a few solitary moments of the morning to gather his thoughts.

He dressed and headed into the kitchen to grab some coffee.

Reginald approached him and handed him a small white envelope. "You're going on a trip today, boy. I need you to go back to Lysallis on your own and deliver this envelope to Mr. Nokei. It must get to him and him only, understand?"

"Yes, sir."

Reginald smiled at him for a moment. "I see you enjoyed yourself last night."

Jonathan took a sip of coffee and let the warm liquid coat

his throat.

Reginald put his hand on Jonathan's shoulder. "Listen, Jonathan, I don't know why anyone in their right mind would ever want to throw away an opportunity like the one you have. You have a beautiful woman you are about to marry, you have access to all the credits you can possibly imagine, and a large, glorious roof over your head. All you have to do is go along with the program that's been set up."

"I am very grateful for everything you have done."

Reginald smiled and then shook his finger at him. "I wish I could believe you, my boy, but I still have my doubts. I need you to prove yourself to me. That will be your goal between now and the wedding tomorrow."

Jonathan shrugged. "How do I prove myself to you?" He took another sip of coffee, knowing this was going to get really interesting. He rubbed the envelope in his hand and wondered what was inside it. It felt extremely thin, whatever it was, but he knew it would be a mistake to open it.

"You'll find a way, I am sure. Or maybe I will." Reginald turned to walk away. "The limo will be here in a half hour to take you to the airport. Dress your best. Mr. Nokei does not care for orphans. I will have a car take Christina home after she wakes up."

***

A couple hours later, Jonathan stood in front of the door to Mr. Nokei's lobby, debating on how to enter. He knew Rebecca would be sitting at the front desk, and all of his feelings for her would spark up again. He had to control his emotions. He took a deep breath and focused. He just had to go in, hand the envelope to Mr. Nokei, and then leave. This would be one way to show Reginald that he could be trusted.

Jonathan walked into the lobby staring straight toward the office doors at the other end. He approached the counter and, with some relief, noticed a different female behind the computer. She was older and had chains linked to her glasses that wrapped around her neck.

"May I help you?"

He let out a sigh and nodded, holding the envelope in his hands. "Yes, I need to see Mr. Nokei."

Her fingers raced across the keyboard while she squinted at the monitor. "Mr. Nokei does not have any appointments at this time. He is out of the office until five this afternoon. Would you like to come back then?"

Jonathan glanced down at his watch. It was two o'clock. That would leave him three hours to wander Lysallis. He figured it would give him a chance to unwind, maybe stop by a bar and get something to relax his nerves and prevent him from thinking so much.

"Sure, I'll be back at five."

The woman nodded and flashed her dentures at him. "See you in a bit."

Jonathan turned and started to head out of the lobby when someone grabbed his waist from behind. He turned quickly on reflex and stumbled back. Rebecca waved an envelope in front of her.

"Wha-wha-what are you doing here?"

"Silly, I work here, if you haven't forgotten already. I have the day off, but I came by to pick up my paycheck."

He smiled nervously at her and decided he better leave. "Nice seeing you. I have to go." He turned and pulled the door open to the hallway.

"So soon? Mr. Nokei won't be back until five. Would you like to go somewhere together?"

"Um, no. No, I'll be fine on my own. I have some spots I…uh…need to check out for my guardians."

"Oh, Reginald?"

"Yeah, Reginald."

"I didn't really care for him, Huxley, and I don't think you do either. He interrupted us. We can pick up where we left off if you'd like."

Jonathan's heart raced with anticipation, but he shook his head and stepped into the hallway. "I'm sorry, Rebecca, but I really have to go." He started down the corridor, refusing to turn around.

"You don't have to. Your choice is to leave. You always have a choice, you know."

He stopped near the elevators, debating on pushing the button. What happened to his freedom of choice? Had it been stripped when he agreed to marry into Christina's lunatic family? He realized he was changing for the sole purpose of pleasing someone else.

He sensed Rebecca's presence coming toward him. He pushed the down arrow button and wished for the elevator doors to open so he could escape.

Her hand touched his shoulder and his body went stiff.

"Don't you feel that energy? I felt it when I kissed you that night. It's proof that you and I are made for each other, cut from the same mold, just different souls made to interlock."

He turned toward her with a frown. "As much as I want to be with you, Rebecca, I can't. I have to forget about you, okay? You have to forget about me."

She took her hand off him and nodded. "Very well. You

struck me as the type of guy who didn't let others choose for you. But I guess I was wrong. There's a first time for everything, I suppose."

She started to walk away when the elevator door eased open.

He turned to watch her retreat down the hallway, purposefully slow as if to torture him with her movement. "I am pledged to be married, in order to have the Arthurs as my guardians."

She stopped and turned around. "Ah…another woman? I should have known. No matter, though." She started toward him as the elevator doors began to shut. He stuck his arm in and they jolted back open. He stepped in and pushed the L button, wishing with all his might that the doors would close before—

She rushed into the elevator and grabbed his face in her hands, crushing her lips into his. He grabbed her waist at the curves, felt the smooth cloth of her shirt, her skin warm underneath, and inhaled the lovely rose-scented perfume filling the air.

They pulled apart just as the elevator doors opened to the first floor lobby. She grabbed his hand and yanked him out of the elevator. "Let's have some fun, shall we?"

***

They returned to the tall blue bank building at 4:56p.m., exhausted and excited from the day they'd had at the annual Lysallis Winter Festival. They participated in a snowball fight, rode a small Ferris wheel, drank gingerbread lattes, and made out in the backseat of the city bus. He promised himself he would never forget this day. They took pictures in one of the small photo booths at the festival, a strip of four black-and-white photos: one of them kissing, two of them making funny faces, and one of them in a happy, couples-like pose. He took the last photo for himself and gave the rest to her.

They stepped out of the elevator on Mr. Nokei's floor and started down the hallway.

"Did you have fun?"

Jonathan nodded. "More than I ever have before."

"That's good."

They stopped in front of the door to Mr. Nokei's lobby. She kissed him on the cheek and smiled brightly. "Don't ever let anyone govern how you live. If you were happier on the streets, then maybe that's where you actually belong. I would hate to see your wonderful smile and spirit destroyed because you gave in."

He smiled, not knowing what to say.

She held his arm. "We'll see each other again soon, but it will be up to you, okay? You know where to find me. Don't keep Mr. Nokei waiting," she said as she started down the hallway.

Jonathan entered the lobby. The old woman with chained glasses still sat behind the counter, furiously typing away on the computer.

"I'm back to see Mr. Nokei."

"Yes." She pressed an intercom button on her phone and signaled for the man. His office door opened at the end of the small hallway and he strode out. He wore a dark suit, and his face was engulfed in well-groomed hair. He took the envelope from Jonathan and nodded. Then he went back to his office and Jonathan set off for his return journey to Mecca.

***

Late that night, Rebecca sat in her little apartment in Lysallis, gazing at the city from her window on the seventh floor. Out in the distance, she spotted the tall blue bank building that invaded her weekly life.

She thought of Jonathan and wondered what he was doing. She believed it awful to give so much power of choice to other individuals, strangers at that. She felt sorry for him and yet somehow knew he would make the right decisions, even if it took some time.

She changed into her pajamas and wanted to sleep but couldn't. Her heart raced for Jonathan, and she wanted so badly to see him. She decided that staying up all night wishing for him wouldn't do any good, so she decided to turn in, even if it meant staring at the ceiling all night.

She shut the blinds to the window overlooking the city and turned the radio off. The jazz music hadn't helped either. It only made her wish for Jonathan more. She entered the hallway and started toward her bedroom when she heard what sounded like a scratching noise from the kitchen. Peeking into the kitchen, she saw nothing but the shadows being cast from the small nightlight in the wall.

She turned around toward the hallway and bumped into a figure dressed in all black. She tried to scream, but his hand impacted her face, knocking her to the floor. She clambered across the tile as the masked figure moved quickly toward her, grabbed her ankles and pulled her toward him. He lifted her up by the hips and tossed her into the lower cabinets as dishes from the counter came crashing down around her.

"Help!" Her voice left her throat at such a high velocity that she didn't even hear herself scream. The intruder grabbed her, then turned her back toward him and pulled her close, holding a small knife to her neck.

Tears burst from her eyes at the thought of dying so quickly and violently. Rebecca kicked at the kitchen counter, shoving all of her weight into her assailant. She fell to the floor as he stumbled back and slammed into the hallway wall. Pictures fell and smashed to the ground.

She scrambled to her feet but stumbled a bit, feeling a warmth across her neck. She clasped her palm to her neck, realizing his knife had cut into her, but not deep enough to kill her instantly. She was bleeding, though, and knew she had to get help.

Rebecca crawled up over the kitchen counter and made her way into the living room, but he was already ahead of her. He reached for her and she ducked, shoving all of her weight into his midsection as he crashed into the glass coffee table.

A bit of a dizzy spell come over her, but she regained her balance and managed to get to the front door. She fumbled with the locks and dove into the hallway. With nobody current-ly in the hall, she decided her best chance would be to get outside, into the public. Rebecca swayed down the hallway, bouncing from wall to wall as her blood speckled the tan carpeting. Her vision began to blur, but she managed to move herself to the elevator. She slammed her fist into the buttons, smearing blood across them.

Her attacker tore out of the doorway and barreled down the corridor, charging toward her like a mad bull. Rebecca darted into the stairwell and started to make her way down. But he was too fast and came up right behind her, shoving his weight into her back. She plummeted down the stairs headfirst, tumbling down the small flight and plowing into the wall at the sixth floor. He sprang down the stairs like a jackrabbit and came up over her, pulling his knife on her again.

This time she used all of her strength and brought her leg

up as hard as she could into his groin. He fell to his knees. She used the wall to hoist herself up and then started down the stairs again, her vision blurring even more. She could feel her heartbeat slowing, her breathing coming out in painful pulses, and realized she might not make it.

Rebecca managed to get down to the second floor, but that's when her strength left her completely and she toppled down the stairs.

Chapter 6

The Shadow of Despair

Jonathan sat in the hospital that night—all night—watching over Rebecca as she lay in bed, unconscious. It was a matter of suspicion that someone had thought to contact Reginald, who in turn relayed the information about the accident to Jonathan, but Jonathan figured maybe it had something to do Mr. Nokei or Rebecca's connections to others in the city.

Reginald had agreed to let Jonathan return to Lysallis to pay his respects to her before the wedding. To say his good-byes, in other words.

Jonathan gazed on her helpless body, hoping and willing her to wake up from her coma. He wanted to know who would have done this, who would have sought to kill Rebecca. She was found at the bottom of the stairs in her apartment building in a puddle of her own blood. Someone had apparently tried to slit her throat but managed to accomplish only half a job of it.

A young nurse stepped into the room and went through the process of checking Rebecca's vitals.

"Any word yet?"

She shook her head. "No word. She's still pretty deep in a coma."

Jonathan kept from crying, though unsure how. How could one of the happiest days of his life turn into one of his worst nightmares?

The nurse finished checking Rebecca's vitals and then approached Jonathan, frowning. "Do you know who is going to pay for her hospital care?"

"What do you mean? She works for Mr. Nokei. Won't he take care of it?"

The nurse shook her head. "No, we can find no records of insurance for her through his company."

"Then won't her family take care of it?" Come to think of it, her family hadn't been by the hospital at all.

"She has no family, Mr. Huxley. She is an orphan. The hospital is pulling some funds together from charities in the area, but they won't be near enough to guarantee her hospital assistance for much longer."

An orphan? Like me? "But don't you have to keep her here until she comes out of her coma?"

The nurse shook her head again, this time trying to smile as if it were the polite thing to do. "No, not since that law was passed about a year ago. We have the right to refuse patients after they've been here for a full week. There are too many people in Lysallis to take care of, and we can't have her lying here, taking up room."

"But she's in a coma! Where are you going to send her?"

"The hospital will decide that when the time comes. I just wanted to give you a heads up so you can plan accordingly."

"How much does it cost to keep her here each day?"

"You can't afford it."

"What was that?"

She sighed apologetically. "Look, it's about ten thousand a week to keep her here, okay? There's no way you could afford that, so what's the point of even telling you? Just say your goodbyes and hope to see her on the other side, if there is another side." She walked out of the room, leaving him there with his dying affection.

Jonathan buried his face in his palms and tried to keep himself adjusted. He heard footsteps. When he looked up, he saw Reginald standing there in a long brown coat and brown fedora.

"How is she, Jonathan?"

He shrugged. "I don't know. She's in a coma. The hospital is saying they're going to send her away to who knows where in a week if someone can't come up with the credits to keep her here."

Reginald took his hat off and stared down at the girl for a moment.

"I want to know why anyone would want to kill her. Who would do such a thing?"

Reginald shook his head. "There are different breeds of people in this world, Jonathan. Some like to beat others, some enjoy giving to charity, and yet still, some thirst for blood in ways that no human should. It could have been a random picking. She is attractive—very attractive—making her prey to any sexual predator or sick pervert."

"Can you help her?"

Reginald let out a breath of air that almost sounded like a laugh. "I'm not a doctor. Far from it."

"I meant financially…help with her hospital bills and give her a fighting chance."

Reginald glared at him. "No, my boy, I will not help her. She is not family to me, nor is she family to you. We Arthurs take care of our own, and that is it. That is how we have survived for decades and that is why we will survive for decades more. You, Jonathan, are the key to our family's heritage, and I'm counting on you to pull yourself together and prepare for this wedding."

Jonathan stood up and peered out the window at the falling snow, sudden fear striking his heart at the thought of marrying Christina. What about Rebecca? What if he were to marry Christina only to have Rebecca wake up hours later? *It doesn't matter*, he thought. Rebecca was a good time. This coma was a sign to move on and make the best of what he had left in life, which didn't seem like much to begin with.

Reginald placed his hat back on. "Be home by morning, Jonathan. Tomorrow is the day of your wedding."

***

Later that night, Jonathan found himself at the closest bar to the hospital, a place called the Midnight Brewery. He sat in a booth in the far corner all by himself, drinking pale ale, hoping to drown out the night so he could head home in the morning and move on with his excuse for a life.

Visions of Rebecca haunted his mind and soul. Her touch had sent shockwaves through his system, and he couldn't help but still feel her warm lips pressed against his. He felt tears welling up in his eyes at the inner turmoil inflicting him, but he pushed them back, knowing he had to survive this phase in his life to have any hope for his future.

He took a final chug of ale, cleaning out the mug. He resolved to leave in a few minutes, after he felt his pain numb to a level that would allow him to function properly. A tall man dressed in all black scooted into the booth right across from him and stared at Jonathan.

"Can I help you?"

"I have a business proposition for you."

Jonathan waved him away. "Get lost. I want to be alone."

"I think you may want to hear me out. You see, I know about Rebecca Soft, lying up there in that hospital in a deep coma. I also know about the outrageous amounts of credits it will take to keep her there."

"What's your point? Who are you, anyway?"

"I am a friend of the Shadow."

"The Shadow? What is that, some kinda comic book character?"

The man grinned. "The Shadow is a mercenary slash bounty hunter. He does different things for different people and makes a lot of credits for it. You grew up on the streets, Jonathan, and I think the Shadow can make good use of your skills to make a nice profit for all involved."

"What kinds of different things?"

The man shrugged. "Different things. Some are seedy, and some are downright nasty, but the end justifies the means, right? You want to be there someday when Rebecca Soft wakes up in that hospital bed that you kept her safe and sound in, right?"

Jonathan pushed the mug to the edge of the table and set his hands on his lap. "How do I know I can trust you or this Shadow character?"

The man nodded. "I knew you would ask that. See, I have a simple job for you to do. It requires little risk on your part and little if any on mine. If you accomplish it, I'll pay you. Then we'll move you up to the next level. The Shadow will pick the jobs he hears about on the streets and will decide what you are capable of doing and what he will pass on to other…employees."

"What is this job, and how much does it pay?"

"We need you to steal something: ingredients from a local bottling company."

"What? That sounds really stupid."

"Doesn't matter how it sounds. You will be paid 25,000

credits if you accomplish this. That will pay for two and a half weeks of hospital care for your lovely rose."

"Why would you pay me 25,000 credits to steal ingredients?"

"Syn Soda has been a struggling cola entity for the past five years. They're about to go bankrupt because of Sunshine Cola, their competitor who has monopolized the cola industry for years. Syn Soda is paying top credit for someone to steal Sunshine Cola's ingredient list so they can come back into the market and put Sunshine out of business."

"You have to admit that does sound really stupid."

"Stupid or not, it's a cool twenty-five grand in your pocket. Maybe you can buy yourself some nice clothes too."

Jonathan laughed at the insult. "Yeah, right. Twenty-five grand for the ingredients to a super cola? That's the most ridiculous thing I've ever heard of. Besides, even if it were true, I wouldn't do it. I don't do those things anymore."

"You'd probably like to think that stealing is behind you, wouldn't you, Jonathan? We'd all like to think that there is a good side to us that we can resurrect from the past, but there isn't. You used to be a thief and a bum on the streets, and I'm giving you a chance to get out of that horrible mansion you've found yourself in, go back to doing what you did just to survive, but this time make a lot of credits doing it. Save your friend. Keep her alive until she has a chance to awaken from her coma, and then the two of you can live happily ever after."

Jonathan thought for a moment, his mind buzzed and blurred by the ale. He stood to his feet and stumbled out of the booth. "Sorry, whatever your name is. But, like I said before, I don't do those things anymore."

"I have a feeling, Jonathan, that your heart will soon change your mind."

Chapter 7

The Wedding

The day of the wedding, Jonathan felt sick to his stomach. He had already vomited once after waking up and felt like he was going to do it again. He stood in the study at Christina's house, with Reginald, putting the last few touches on his tuxedo.

Reginald already attempted to give him his own version of a fatherly speech that included what sounded like a threat if Jonathan were to somehow screw this up. Everything that came out of Reginald's mouth seemed to sound like a threat, and Jonathan didn't like that. He was trying his hardest to make the most of the wedding in general, but to have to be constantly coerced into it only made it that much worse.

The discussion about Rebecca's coma had ended there at the hospital the night Reginald came to visit her. Reginald spoke no more about it, and Jonathan figured it would be wise to do the same, seeing how he would probably never see the girl again. He couldn't stand that thought, though, and no matter how far back he pushed the thoughts of Rebecca, he couldn't get her out of his mind completely. It was like a disease now, making him sick, uprooting all of his emotions and causing him to question everything.

A knock on the door startled him. Reginald opened the door to the gray-haired maid.

"Sirs, the bride is ready and will be walking down the garden strip in five minutes."

Reginald nodded and shut the door, turning back toward Jonathan. "It's time, my boy. Time to unite our families, secure my family's heritage, and hand a silver spoon over to you, practically free of charge."

Sure, Jonathan thought, *for the simple price of my soul.* He took a deep breath. This was it.

Reginald put his hand on the boy's back and led him toward the door. "I told you that everything works out for a reason, Jonathan. Remember that rule? All things have a purpose." He opened the door for Jonathan. They started down the hallway toward the patio where the wedding was about to begin. "See, your friend Rebecca found herself in this unfortunate mess so that you and Christina could be together. That's the simple truth, and that is how the universe balances things out. Did I not try to warn you about seeing her? It's a shame what happened, but it won't deter things from playing out the way they should. That's life. That's pain and joy. That is all things."

Jonathan stepped out onto the patio and saw the dozens of people sitting in rows to his left and right, their fancy dresses and black-and-white suits bringing a bit of fashionable splendor to the garden area. Down the brick path in front of him stood the archway to the hedge maze. He would be taken around one side and she would be taken around the other, and they would meet in the middle, at the dragon fountain. There they would be wed without the eyes of all the people. Then they would come back to the patio and celebrate in dance and partying all night, a party Jonathan knew he would have to drown himself in.

He glanced up toward the sunset that was sinking across the horizon like a waterlogged ship. Reginald started him around the left side of the garden, while only a half moment later, Christina and her wheelchair-bound father came around the other side. Christina's mother and Patricia waited in the middle with the official who would marry the young couple.

Jonathan felt sick, sicker than he had this morning. Bile swirled in his stomach, and the touch of Reginald's hand on his shoulder only made it worse. Jonathan felt hot in his tuxedo and suddenly grew claustrophobic in the alleys of the hedge maze. He and Reginald made it through to the center where they found Christina standing in front of the dragon fountain, her bright white dress sweeping along the short, green blades of grass.

She smiled earnestly at Jonathan and then whispered to her mother, "Boy, he cleans up nicely."

Jonathan wanted Rebecca Soft.

He looked at Christina, then at her mother, and at her father sitting in the wheelchair, helpless and unable to escape the terror of his household. But Jonathan wasn't helpless, and he wasn't unable to escape. Rebecca had been right about him having choices.

His eyes scanned the mammoth fountain behind Christina and her mother, and he realized that the statues resembled them: mean, hideous dragons waiting to devour his soul in return for a family name and glorious riches.

He glanced over at Reginald and Patricia. The poor woman was abused by her husband but somehow felt loved by him at the same time. Everyone around him, anyone connected to this family, seemed to be bound in chains, forced to live a tortured existence. He wanted no part of it.

He took a long look at Reginald. This man disgusted Jonathan now more than ever. Reginald had no sympathy for anyone, no caring at all, no emotions except anger, malice, and spite. He tried to spread his poison to anyone and everyone he came in contact with, but Jonathan was going to put a stop to it. He felt a tinge of regret, at having left his existence with the city gears underneath Mecca. But then he realized he never would have met Rebecca had he not come out of that life.

He took a few steps back from everyone and then smiled. "I can't do this." He looked at Christina when he said it.

Her eyes grew darker than he had ever seen them, striking a chord of fear in him. But he overcame it for the moment and turned and headed back through the hedge maze, determined to do what was necessary, not just for his survival, but also for his own happiness.

Chapter 8

Jonathan's Syns

J onathan sat in the same bar in Lysallis, same booth that night, clad in the white dress shirt and black slacks of the morning's event.

The man from the night before, clad in black once again, displayed a cocky grin on his face like he had the last time Jonathan had spoken to him. "Okay, listen, we need those ingredients tonight."

"Tonight?" Jonathan shook his head. "No way. I've had a long day as it is. I can start on it tomorrow if you want."

"Tonight, and we throw in an extra 5,000 credits, rounding out another half a week you can keep your love in the hospital if you so choose."

"How do you propose I go about stealing these ingredients?"

"They're in the batch mixer's office in the Sunshine Cola factory on the east side of Lysallis. They don't keep it under high security. That would only alert people to where the ingredients are. They're in a wall safe behind the picture of soda vat number five. The combination to the lock is six, twelve, seventy-nine."

"How the blazes do you know all of this?"

The man smiled arrogantly. "Don't worry about it. Just do this quickly. Bring me back the ingredients in the next few hours, and I'll throw in a piece of valuable information that I've managed to come across."

Jonathan attempted to rub the tiredness from his eyes. The man placed a small suitcase down beside Jonathan's legs. "This is in case you need them." Then he stood up. "I'll be back here a little later. A car is waiting outside to take you to the factory." Then he left the bar.

Jonathan lifted the suitcase onto the table, glancing around to make sure nobody was staring intently at him. He flipped it open and found a small, rectangular box, which he quickly recognized as a lock pick kit. He had always wanted one of these high-end ones when he lived on the streets. Next to the box, cushioned in the deep velvet lining of the suitcase, lay a shiny, silver pistol. He dreaded the thought of having to kill anyone, especially in cold blood, but he figured it was just a contingency measure meant for his own safety. Near the pistol he found a pair of black leather gloves.

He shut the case and headed out the door to the waiting car.

***

A half hour later, the car dropped him off in front of the mammoth Sunshine Cola factory. His ride then sped away into the dark shadows surrounding the facility, leaving him there alone. He gazed up at the building, marveling at the large cisterns that rose up above the three-story factory at the center of the property.

He had slipped on the black leather gloves while in the car. They were a perfect fit, as if the one who had purchased them had somehow measured Jonathan's hands before.

Jonathan found it easy to avoid detection as he snuck through the guard station and past the rent-a-cop guards. Using the new lock pick kit, he gained access into the building. He even avoided the cameras with ease.

He reached the office fast enough. It was a small room, plainly decorated with a small wooden desk and pictures of different areas of the factory hanging on the walls. He found the picture of soda vat number five and even got the combination lock open in record time. Inside the safe, he found stacks and stacks of credits. He debated on taking these, his conscience kicking in, but then he decided that since it was to save a girl's life, it was okay. He shoved the wads of credits into his pockets. Then he dug into the safe for the yellow index card encased in a glass molding.

"Hold it right there!"

He froze in place, cursing himself for taking so long. He shoved the yellow card in his back pocket and turned around. A man in a gray suit stood in front of him, holding a shotgun pointed directly at Jonathan.

"Put them back in the safe, all the credits and my ingredients. Now!"

Jonathan observed the man for a moment, sizing him up. He stood about six feet tall and had a five o'clock shadow. He looked tired and worn out, and his wide eyes showed desperation and panic in them. His hands trembled while holding the shotgun. This guy wasn't exactly a pro. But then again, neither was Jonathan.

"You're the third one this week to try and take those from me. Now, put them back!"

"The third?"

"Yeah. The third thief to try and rob me of my livelihood. Those ingredients have been passed down from generations of hard workers like me, and you're not getting out of here with them."

Jonathan slowly started to pull the pistol from the back of his waistband. The man noticed and came closer, shoving the pair of shotgun barrels into Jonathan's chest.

"If you move another inch, I'll blow a hole through you the size of Lysallis, do you hear me?"

Jonathan nodded. Then, in a quick motion, he grabbed the barrels of the shotgun and shoved the weapon upward. A shot fired, jolting the gun and knocking them both to the floor. Ceiling pieces came raining down on them as Jonathan scrambled to find the weapon. The man took a moment to recollect himself...a moment too long. Jonathan already had the shotgun up and pointed in the man's face.

"P-p-please don't hurt me. J-just take what you want, okay? But please, leave the ingredients. That's the only source of our success. This company has been in my family for so long, I can't bear to let it go to the likes of Syn Soda. I've gone so long without selling out to them, and I don't want to begin now."

Jonathan struggled with this information, just long enough for the man to grab the barrel of the shotgun to do what Jonathan had done moments earlier. But Jonathan's reflexes were too quick, and another shot fired, blowing the man backward in a mist of blood.

Jonathan dropped the gun and darted to the man's side. He lay on his back, his hands holding his torn chest. He muttered something Jonathan couldn't understand, and then after a few moments, he stopped moving and his eyes closed.

Jonathan stood to his feet and slammed his back against the wall near the safe, his eyes wide with terror. Had he just killed a man? He had never killed before, had never really needed to. Usually on the streets, nobody had enough to kill each other over, and the only fights that really occurred were over stale food and the women who wandered the alleys.

He closed his eyes and wished it all away. He wished he hadn't taken this stupid job. He wished he hadn't agreed to the Arthurs' terms of surrender. He wished he hadn't met Rebecca. His heart ached for her and pained for this poor dead man.

Jonathan took control of his emotions as best he could, realizing with terrible complexity that for this man to die so Rebecca could live justified it. He opened his eyes and picked up the murder weapon, thankful he had worn gloves and avoided all of the security cameras, meaning nobody would know he had done this. Nobody but the Shadow and the Shadow's accomplice, who had set this whole thing up.

Jonathan left the Sunshine Cola factory the same way he entered. The car was waiting for him outside, and it drove him and the ingredients back to the bar. When he arrived, he found the gentleman dressed in all black already sitting at the booth, a wide smile on his face.

Jonathan slid into the booth, yellow ingredients card in hand.

"You did good." The man took the ingredients list from Jonathan and handed him an envelope in return. Jonathan opened it to find a bundle of credits. His heart jumped at the possibilities for Rebecca and him, pushing the death of the factory worker to the back of his mind, at least for the moment.

"There's forty thousand there, Jonathan."

He looked up from the envelope. "Forty?"

The man nodded with that same cocky smile on his face. "Another objective of yours was to kill Gregory Izbech, the factory owner."

"What? I didn't...I didn't sign up to kill anyone."

"I know. You wouldn't have been able to if you knew you were doing it ahead of time, since you haven't killed anyone before. I called Gregory and told him what you were doing and knew there would be a confrontation. I had faith that you would be able to accomplish the task, and there in your hands is your reward for it."

Jonathan didn't know what to say. He wanted to argue the point, to lash out at this man for the treachery involved in what had happened, but the credits in his hands quieted his spirit. All he could seem to think of was Rebecca lying in that hospital bed, her sweet soul calling out to him to save her.

"Now that you accomplished your assignment, I have a piece of information that may drive you forward in your quest to avenge what happened to your precious Rebecca."

Jonathan stuffed the credits into his pocket with the currency he stole from the factory and stared at the man for a moment. "What are you talking about?" The man's smile was driving Jonathan crazy. He almost wanted to shoot this man himself and then see if he would have the same arrogant smear across his face.

"Reginald Arthur placed the hit on Rebecca Soft."

Jonathan's body tensed at the mention of the name.

"Reginald Arthur set up the hit to kill Rebecca. Obviously, she fought back and the hit didn't go off as planned. Now she's in a coma, all because of your guardian."

"Reginald?" He let the information process in his reeling mind. Reginald hated Rebecca, hated anyone other than Christina. He would have done anything to keep the family name intact, even if it meant killing Rebecca. "Who was the assailant?"

The man shook his head. "I don't have that much information. All I've been able to find out for you is who set it up.

Nobody on the streets knows who actually attempted the hit, and whoever did it isn't going to brag about it because it was a botched and quite humiliating attempt at that."

Jonathan suddenly felt his whole world crumbling. He had walked out of the wedding, meaning now he could never return to Reginald's circle. His home and his shelter were gone. He couldn't return to living out of trash cans either, not after this last week of living in practical royalty. He had only one choice. His gaze moved across the table and rested on the man seated on the other side.

"Yes, I have more jobs for you. There's an abundance, and the Shadow and I have the best connections. You keep doing good work like tonight, and you'll move up in the ranks pretty fast. I can teach you what I know, help you with some areas you might be weak in. I can show you all the new technology that's out there on the streets and give you access to it all to accomplish your jobs. Stick with the Shadow, and you'll be well-off in no time."

"I need to meet him."

The man put his fingers to his forehead and scratched an invisible itch. "Excuse me?"

"I want to meet the Shadow."

He shook his head. "Nobody meets the shadow, kiddo. He lives in darkness, and nobody has ever seen his face and lived to tell of it."

"How can I trust you and this Shadow if I've never met him?"

"The credits are the trust. You did a job out of good faith and you were paid well for it. That's how trust among the three of us will be generated."

"What's the next job?"

"I'll contact you. Find a place to lie low for a couple days, let the heat on this Sunshine Cola job die down. Go be with your Rebecca."

"No. I think I'm going to pay the Arthurs a visit."

The man shook his head adamantly. "No, you won't. That's a big, big mistake. Reginald Arthur is so well-connected, to the likes of Mr. Big and even Mr. Nokei. You don't want to mess with Reginald. You ditched his wedding plans, and that's bad enough. Lie low, let things cool off, and we'll contact you with the next job. If you go after Reginald, you pretty much take your own life into your hands. Let it be. He wasn't the one who actually tried to kill Rebecca. Maybe your efforts would be better spent trying to figure that out while you wait for her to wake up from her coma."

Jonathan knew the man had a point. "Very well."

Chapter 9

Death and Birth

J onathan decided the best place to lie low would be
Lysallis, since that was where Rebecca was anyway. He
took some of his credits and rented a small apartment.
Instead of visiting the hospital, he decided to go to the scene of
the crime, back to Rebecca's apartment. He wanted to see if he
could find a clue as to who had tried to kill her, something to
go on in his quest for revenge.

He arrived at her building and took the elevator to the seventh floor. When the doors opened, he noticed dark blood
marring the carpet in the hallway. *That was her blood*, he thought.
It made him ill. He followed the trail to a door at the end of
the corridor. Yellow strips of caution tape made an X over the
doorway, and a note on the door declared this a crime scene
involved in an ongoing investigation. Jonathan tightened the
black gloves and used his new lock pick kit to break into the
apartment, shutting and locking the door behind him.

He found the entryway dark, but moving around the corner
to the living room, he saw the city lights breaking through a
crack in the curtains. He pulled them open and peered out on
the city. The tall blue bank building sat in the distance like a

beacon to remind him of where he had met Rebecca.

He made his way into the kitchen. Turning the light on, he saw spots of blood across the tile floor. The blood led over the counter and into the living room, and he figured this must have been where she had struggled with her attacker. *You were so strong,* he thought, *to have lasted so long against someone so intent on ending your life.*

He almost cried at the thought of a person wanting to kill someone so precious, so innocent. He shook the feelings away and scanned the kitchen floor. A piece of fabric looked like it had been ripped off in the scuffle. He picked it up and examined it, noticing it was a material he had never seen before.

He stuck it in his pocket, knowing the police would never get around to investigating it, and then made his way back to the bedroom. It was a large room with a canopy bed and maroon-colored walls. The black wood furniture gave him a sense of happiness as he thought about Rebecca waking up and sharing her life with him. He would make sure to move her out of this place and into his apartment, where he could keep her safe from harm.

***

On the other side of town, in the hospital, Rebecca's body lay motionless, except for her chest, which rose and fell with each breath she took. The coma held its reign over her and trapped her in her subconsciousness.

A dark figure loomed over her bed…a figure that didn't belong there.

"I tried before, dear Rebecca, and I failed. But I won't fail now, because you can't fight back this time. You took my family name from me, my riches, my would-be husband. Now

I will take from you what is rightfully mine."

In her mind, Rebecca screamed for Jonathan, for someone to save her. But it was no use. She could neither speak nor move.

Christina Harbrook came into the light. She wore a black dress, and a black veil was pulled back from her face. She carried an expensive black, gator-skin purse. She bent over the bed and held a small black cloth over Rebecca's face. She held it there until the machines keeping Rebecca alive started wailing out across the room, like banshees screaming for freedom from their spiritual prisons. A flat line appeared on the EKG monitor, and Christina removed the cloth, stuffing it back into her purse. Then she draped the black veil over her face and walked out of the hospital room, passing the nurse station on her way toward the elevator.

The nurses were already frantic over the alerts the machines were giving off. Some rushed right past her to get into the room she had just left.

Christina hit the down elevator button. As the doors slid open, she stepped in.

***

After surveying Rebecca's apartment, Jonathan decided to head to the hospital to see her before turning in for the night. As he arrived there, a sudden sense of doom began to consume him.

He approached the elevators of the quiet lobby and pressed the up button. Glancing around, he didn't notice anything out of the ordinary. He saw a nurse or two walking around with charts, and a couple of male nurses carting an emergency victim in from an ambulance outside.

The elevator doors slid open and a woman in a black veil

stepped out and passed him. Had he been less eager to see Rebecca, he may have thought the woman to be out of place at that moment in time. But instead of pondering that, he stepped into the elevator, immediately overcome by the scent of dark chocolate. He took the elevator up. When the doors opened to Rebecca's floor, mass chaos greeted him. Nurses were scurrying around in a panic, and a couple of doctors were standing at the entrance to Rebecca's room.

Jonathan shoved his way past the staff and entered the room, rushing to the bed. He gazed at Rebecca's peaceful face and knew with morbid clarity that she was alive no more. He bent over and kissed her on the lips as tears streamed from his eyes. He smelled her beautiful rose scent, and it made him cry even more.

There on the hospital bed he felt his own life end.

Some nurses approached him, placing their hands on his shoulders, hoping to comfort him. But instead of taking their empathy, he pushed their embraces away. When his face turned toward them, it showed nothing but rage.

"How did she die?! How did she die in a hospital?!"

The head doctor approached him. "Young man, she was in a steady coma on the right equipment. There's no reason she should have passed in this manner. Yes, it is possible for her body to just give up, but we suspect foul play."

Jonathan stared at the man in silence, save for his heavy breathing. Jonathan turned back to Rebecca's body and felt more tears stream out of his eyes. He decided to let it all come, let all the emotions he had held back for so long out so he could get it over with. He never wanted to feel this pain again, this heartache that threatened to steal his soul and crush it into dust.

He heard the nurses talking behind him, and when he turned back around, he noticed that some police officers had arrived. He decided this would be a good time to go.

He kissed his fingers and gently brushed them across Rebecca's forehead. He turned to leave, shoving his way out of the room, past the cops, and back to the elevator.

"Hey! Where are you going? These officers have some questions for you."

When the elevator doors slammed shut, Jonathan started his descent.

***

Jonathan found himself at the Lysallis Cemetery days later to see the burial for his beloved Rebecca. He anonymously paid for the funeral costs and the plot. He couldn't bear for her not to get a proper departure from this hideous world.

Over the past couple days, he managed to get his thoughts together in a calculating manner. He decided he didn't want to work solely for the Shadow. He couldn't trust anyone anymore, not even himself. He realized that Reginald Arthur would have to be dealt with, in time, but the real person he wanted to find was the one who had attempted to kill Rebecca and then finished the job at the hospital.

The image of the lady in the black veil kept entering his mind. He found it strange that she was wearing a veil in a hospital and he couldn't help but wonder if she had anything to do with Rebecca's untimely death. He didn't want to jump to conclusions about the woman or pursue a dead end, but neither did he want to ignore his feelings and observations about her.

He decided that the only important thing to him now was to find Rebecca's killer. If it killed him in the process, then it would only put him out of his misery. He was glued to this life of crime now, and there was no way around it.

He resolved that he would work on his own, as a freelance mercenary, doing odd jobs for anyone on the streets to continue to bring in funds to support his cause. He knew people who needed things done, having lived on the streets most of his life. He would work for the Shadow every now and then, but overall he wanted to stay in charge of his own life at this point.

He also set up a list of rules for his jobs to help him avoid any unnecessary deaths or destruction that some of these tasks might attract. He would not kill anyone unless it was absolutely necessary to the job at hand. He would do whatever job came his way if it paid enough, because finding Rebecca's killer was his highest priority now.

He stood behind a tree, listening to the official speak of Rebecca as if he had known her personally. Dark and foreboding clouds drifted swiftly in the sky like dead bodies sliding across an icy lake. Rebecca's burial had gathered a small group of people, most of them friends, some work associates. Even Mr. Nokei had come. He stood stoic with no expression on his woman he loved, but he couldn't risk being seen with Rebecca's killer on the loose and the Arthurs wallowing in anger at his blatant disrespect for their family heritage.

He pulled a small black-and-white photo from his pocket, the one of him and Rebecca at the Winter Festival. Flipping the photo over, he saw the stamp of "Drather Photography" in faint gray ink. He remembered that the photo booth had the name Drather Photography on it. *Drather*…he twirled the name around in his mind, tried it on for size.

He decided to change his name to Drather, no longer wanting to be Jonathan Huxley, no longer wanting to be a victim.